For Rudi

This book belongs to:

_____

Be nice to this book.

Library of Congress Cataloging-in-Publication Data
available upon request

Copyright © 1994 Coppenrath Verlag, Münster
English-language translation and compilation copyright © 1994 Abbeville Press
ISBN 1-55859-887-1
Story by Ingrid Huber
Illustrations by Constanza Droop
Translated by Laura Lindgren

First edition
4 6 8 10 9 7 5 3

Sleep Tight, Little Bear

Story by Ingrid Huber
Illustrations by Constanza Droop

Abbeville Kids
A DIVISION OF ABBEVILLE PRESS
NEW YORK   LONDON   PARIS

There once was a little bear who lived in a forest in the land of Nowhere. Every day he played with the other animals in the forest and was happy and content. But one day when it got dark and the other animals went home, his little bear eyes didn't want to close.

He simply could not fall asleep.

He tried lying on his left side, then on his right. He tried lying on his back and then on his stomach. Nothing helped at all. Little Bear just could not go to sleep. And so he was sooo tired!

Finally Little Bear got up and ran deep into the
dark forest. Maybe he would find someone there
who could help him fall asleep.

Boom! He wasn't looking, and he bumped smack into a tree.

"Ow!" cried the tree. "Who is waking me up in the middle of the night?"

"Oh, tree," Little Bear cried, "I cannot fall asleep. Whatever shall I do?"

"Oh, I can help you with that," said the tree.

He shook himself a little, and a shower of golden brown leaves fell to the ground.

"You can surely sleep on these," said the tree, and immediately he started snoring again.

Little Bear curled up on the pile of leaves. But—whenever he moved, the leaves rustled. That meant they rustled all the time. And so Little Bear still could not fall asleep.

He went farther and farther. He came to a pond in the forest that shone like a mirror in the moonlight.

What was that suddenly jumping in front of his feet? A grass green frog!

"Oh, frog," said Little Bear, "I cannot fall asleep. Can you tell me what to do?"

"Rrribbit, rrribbit," said the frog. "Lie down on this big lily pad. You can surely sleep there."

"Thank you," said Little Bear.

Carefully he crawled onto the leaf. Goodness, it was wobbly. Every time Little Bear moved, the lily pad rocked back and forth. And so Little Bear still could not fall asleep.

Little Bear went farther and farther into the forest and finally came upon a foxhole.

"Oh, fox!" he cried into the hole, "I cannot fall asleep. Can you tell me what to do?"

"Of course," said the fox, and he came out of his hole. "Come sleep in here. I have to leave anyway."

No sooner had the fox spoken than he had disappeared.

Little Bear crawled headfirst into the foxhole.
But when he got to the end, his bear feet were still
sticking out. And soon they were ice cold.

So Little Bear tried it the other way around.
And what do you think? Now his head was peeking
out of the hole, and Little Bear still could not fall
asleep.

Little Bear went deeper and deeper into the forest. Next he met an owl who sat high on a branch and looked at him with big eyes.

"Hoooo!" cried the owl. "Hoooo!"

"Oh, owl," said Little Bear, "I cannot fall asleep. Do you know what I can do?"

"Yes," said the owl. "Sleep in my nest in this tree. There you will be warm and safe."

"Thank you," said Little Bear, and he climbed into the owl's nest. Unfortunately the owl kept calling out "hoooo!" into the forest, over and over. And so Little Bear still could not fall asleep.

Little Bear wandered and wandered. But he couldn't find anyone else to ask for help. Only high in the sky the moon shone round and bright.

"Oh, moon," Little Bear called out, "I cannot fall asleep. Not in the leaves and not in the foxhole. Not on the lily pad and not in the owl's nest. Whatever shall I do?"

The moon smiled gently and said, "Go a little farther, Little Bear, until you reach the end of the forest. Come, I will light the way. Then you will see where you can sleep."

The forest came to an end and suddenly there were houses all around. They all had dark windows and looked as though they were fast asleep.

All except one. There a warm, inviting, bright light shone from one window onto the street.

Curious, Little Bear went up to it and looked in. On the other side of the bright window in the little house a child sat crying on the bed.

"Hello," said Little Bear. "Can't you fall asleep either?"

"No," said the child, "not at all. And especially not all alone."

"Oh," said Little Bear. "Then why don't I come in and join you."

Happily Little Bear snuggled up with the child,
and the child snuggled up with Little Bear.

And a little while later, when the moon shone through the window, both were sound asleep.

The moon smiled and whispered, "Good night, Little Bear. Good night, child. Sleep tight and pleasant dreams to you both."